P9-ELS-226

GOOD DRIVING, AMELIA BEDELIA

Other Books in the
AMELIA BEDELIA *Series by*
Peggy Parish
from Avon Camelot

AMELIA BEDELIA AND THE BABY
AMELIA BEDELIA GOES CAMPING
AMELIA BEDELIA HELPS OUT
AMELIA BEDELIA'S FAMILY ALBUM
GOOD WORK, AMELIA BEDELIA
MERRY CHRISTMAS, AMELIA BEDELIA

HERMAN PARISH grew up with Amelia Bedelia. He was in the fourth grade when his aunt, Peggy Parish, wrote the first book about everyone's favorite literal-minded housekeeper. Since then he has graduated from the University of Pennsylvania, served as a naval officer, married, had three children (who are Amelia Bedelia fans), and worked for many years as a writer in advertising. He and his family live in San Francisco.

LYNN SWEAT is known and loved by children everywhere as the illustrator of many of Peggy Parish's "Amelia Bedelia" books. Mr. Sweat is a painter as well as an illustrator of children's books, and his paintings hang in galleries across the country. He and his wife live in Connecticut.

Avon Books are available at special quantity discounts for bulk purchases for sales promotions, premiums, fund raising or educational use. Special books, or book excerpts, can also be created to fit specific needs.

For details write or telephone the office of the Director of Special Markets, Avon Books, Dept. FP, 1350 Avenue of the Americas, New York, New York 10019, 1-800-238-0658.

GOOD DRIVING, AMELIA BEDELIA

HERMAN PARISH

Pictures by Lynn Sweat

AN AVON  CAMELOT BOOK

If you purchased this book without a cover, you should be aware that this book is stolen property. It was reported as "unsold and destroyed" to the publisher, and neither the author nor the publisher has received any payment for this "stripped book."

AVON BOOKS
A division of
The Hearst Corporation
1350 Avenue of the Americas
New York, New York 10019

Text copyright © 1995 by Herman S. Parish III
Illustrations copyright © 1995 by Lynn Sweat
Published by arrangement with William Morrow and Company, Inc.
Library of Congress Catalog Card Number: 94-4112
ISBN: 0-380-72510-X
RL: 1.5

All rights reserved, which includes the right to reproduce this book or portions thereof in any form whatsoever except as provided by the U.S. Copyright Law. For information address Permissions Department, William Morrow and Company, Inc., 1350 Avenue of the Americas, New York, New York 10019.

First Avon Camelot Printing: May 1996

CAMELOT TRADEMARK REG. U.S. PAT. OFF. AND IN OTHER COUNTRIES, MARCA REGISTRADA, HECHO EN U.S.A.

Printed in the U.S.A.

QH 10 9 8 7 6 5 4 3

FOR PEGGY PARISH,
THE REAL AMELIA BEDELIA
— H. P.

FOR KEVIN PHILLIP
AND AMANDA LYNN
— L. S.

GOOD DRIVING, AMELIA BEDELIA

Amelia Bedelia walked into the kitchen.
Mr. and Mrs. Rogers sang out,
"Happy Birthday, Amelia Bedelia!"
"Thank you," said Amelia Bedelia.
"Take the day off to celebrate,"
said Mrs. Rogers.

"I'll go and visit my cousin Alcolu,"
said Amelia Bedelia.
"Use our car," said Mr. Rogers.
"Oh, I have not driven in years,"
said Amelia Bedelia.

"Is your license still good?"
asked Mrs. Rogers.
"It's great!" said Amelia Bedelia.
"See how nice my picture looks."

"Your license is fine," said Mr. Rogers.
"Let's see if your driving is as good
as your picture. Meet me at the car.
A short drive in the country
will do you good."

They backed out of the driveway
and away they went.
Amelia Bedelia drove very carefully.

"What a beautiful farm," said Mr. Rogers.

"Yes," said Amelia Bedelia.

"And what a nice bunch of cows."

"*Herd* of cows," said Mr. Rogers.

"Heard of cows?" asked Amelia Bedelia.

"Of course I have heard of cows."

"No," said Mr. Rogers.

"I mean a cow *herd*."

"So what if a cow heard?"
said Amelia Bedelia.

"I didn't say anything bad."

Some cows had wandered onto the road.

"Watch out!" said Mr. Rogers.

Amelia Bedelia stopped the car.

"Steer straight ahead," said Mr. Rogers.

"No," said Amelia Bedelia.

"The steer is behind us."

A cow with big horns looked into the car.
"Push on the horn," said Mr. Rogers.
Amelia Bedelia gently pushed
on the cow's horn.
MOOOOOOOOOOOOOOOO!

Mr. Rogers pushed hard
on the car's horn.
HOOOOOOOOOOOOOOONK!
The cows ran back into the field.

Mr. Rogers took out a road map.

"I am looking for a crossroad," he said.

"It will have signs to tell us where to go."

"While you look, I'll go for a walk,"
said Amelia Bedelia.

"Get some directions if you can,"
said Mr. Rogers.

Amelia Bedelia was back in five minutes.

"I did not find a cross road," she said.

"They were all very nice.

But I got lots of directions.

Would you like a 'North' or a 'South'?

And I have a nice 'Southeast.'"

"*Now* we are lost," said Mr. Rogers.

"I have no idea where we are!"

"I know where we are," said
Amelia Bedelia.

"We are right here."

Mr. Rogers looked back at his map.

They got back in the car.

"Should I look for another nice road?"
asked Amelia Bedelia.

"Don't you dare," said Mr. Rogers.

"Look for a fork in the road."

"I once looked for a needle in a haystack,"
said Amelia Bedelia.

"I never did find it."

Mr. Rogers pointed straight ahead.
"There is the fork," he said.
Amelia Bedelia looked very hard.
She saw that the road split
into two roads.

"Which road is the fork in?"
asked Amelia Bedelia.

"This road," said Mr. Rogers.

"I don't see any forks or spoons,"
said Amelia Bedelia.

"Which way should I turn?"

"Turn left," said Mr. Rogers.

"Left?" asked Amelia Bedelia.

"Right," said Mr. Rogers.

"Okay, I will turn right,"
said Amelia Bedelia.

"Not *right*," said Mr. Rogers.

"Right is *not* right!"

"Well, right is not left,"
said Amelia Bedelia.

"That's right," said Mr. Rogers.
"Left *is* right! Right is *wrong*!"
"I am really mixed up,"
said Amelia Bedelia.
"Right is wrong? Left is right?
Which way should I turn?"

"Bear left!" shouted Mr. Rogers.
So Amelia Bedelia made a sharp turn...
to the right.

"Amelia Bedelia!" shouted Mr. Rogers.

"Why did you turn right?"

"Because," said Amelia Bedelia,

"you warned me about the bear."

"*What* bear?" asked Mr. Rogers.

"You said there was a bear

on the left," said Amelia Bedelia.

"There was no *bear*!" yelled Mr. Rogers.

"I said bear *left*."

"Oh," said Amelia Bedelia.

"If I'd known that the bear had left,

I would not have turned right."

Mr. Rogers was about to blow up.
The tire beat him to it.

KAAAAA-POWIE!
Thump! Thump! Thump!

"A flat tire!" said Mr. Rogers.
He got out to put on the spare.
Mr. Rogers opened the trunk.
He let out a big yell.

"What's wrong?" asked Amelia Bedelia.
"Did that bear come back?"

"Where is the spare tire?"
said Mr. Rogers.
"And where is the jack?"
"I don't know where Jack went,"
said Amelia Bedelia.
"Mrs. Rogers took everything
out of the trunk yesterday.
She said she had a lot to buy
at the party store."

Mr. Rogers let out a sigh.

"This has been a long drive in the country," said Amelia Bedelia.

"The walk back to town will be even longer," said Mr. Rogers. "Stay here. I'll go and get help."

"Good luck," said Amelia Bedelia.

Mr. Rogers disappeared down the road.

Minutes later Amelia Bedelia

heard something coming.

It was not Mr. Rogers.

It was not even a car.

It was a tow truck.

"Need any help?" asked the driver.

"That depends," said Amelia Bedelia.

"Are you a Jack?"

"My name is John," he said.

"But you can call me Jack for short."

"I don't care how tall you are,"

said Amelia Bedelia.

"If you are a Jack, you'll do."

Jack looked at the flat tire.

He pulled out a big nail.

"Here is your problem," said Jack.

"A nail?" said Amelia Bedelia.

"I thought I ran over a fork in the road."

Jack smiled. "Do you have a spare tire?"

"I'd like to give you one,"
said Amelia Bedelia.

"But we don't have enough good tires
for ourselves."

Jack smiled again.

"Would you like me to give you a tow?"

"I've got all the toes I need,"

said Amelia Bedelia.

"But could you pull our car

back to town?"

"Good idea," said Jack.
He hooked up the car.
They drove down the road
and picked up Mr. Rogers.
Then they headed for home.

There was a big crowd
outside the Rogers house.
"Looks like a party," said Jack.
"How wonderful!" said Amelia Bedelia.

Mr. Rogers got out of the truck.

"Good heavens!" said Mrs. Rogers.

"You look run down!"

"Don't say that around Amelia Bedelia,"
said Mr. Rogers. "She might do it."

"Happy Birthday, Amelia Bedelia!"
said Cousin Alcolu.

"Hello, Cousin Alcolu,"
said Amelia Bedelia.

"Mr. Rogers was helping me practice
my driving so I could come to see you.
But we didn't get very far."

"That's okay," said Cousin Alcolu.

"I can drive. I can come to see you
anytime you want.
You will not have to drive at all."

Mr. Rogers shook his hand.
"Thank you, Cousin Alcolu.
It may be Amelia Bedelia's birthday,
but you just gave me the
best present ever."

Amelia Bedelia cut giant slices
of birthday cake for everyone.
And nobody had to go out
to the road to find a fork.

JOIN THE FUN
WITH LITERAL-MINDED

AMELIA BEDELIA

BY PEGGY PARISH
Pictures by Lynn Sweat

AMELIA BEDELIA'S FAMILY ALBUM
71698-4/$3.99 US/$4.99 CAN

AMELIA BEDELIA AND THE BABY
72795-1/$3.99 US/$4.99 CAN

AMELIA BEDELIA HELPS OUT
53403/$3.99 US/$5.50 CAN

GOOD WORK, AMELIA BEDELIA
72831-1/$3.99 US/$4.99 CAN

AMELIA BEDELIA GOES CAMPING
70067-0/$3.99 US/$5.50 CAN

MERRY CHRISTMAS, AMELIA BEDELIA
70325-4/$3.99 US/$5.50 CAN

BY HERMAN PARISH
GOOD DRIVING, AMELIA BEDELIA
72510-X/$3.99 US/$5.50 CAN

Buy these books at your local bookstore or use this coupon for ordering:

Mail to: Avon Books, Dept BP, Box 767, Rte 2, Dresden, TN 38225   E
Please send me the book(s) I have checked above.
❏ My check or money order—no cash or CODs please—for $_____is enclosed (please
add $1.50 per order to cover postage and handling—Canadian residents add 7% GST).
❏ Charge my VISA/MC Acct#_____Exp Date_____
Minimum credit card order is two books or $7.50 (please add postage and handling
charge of $1.50 per order—Canadian residents add 7% GST). For faster service, call
1-800-762-0779. Residents of Tennessee, please call 1-800-633-1607. Prices and numbers are
subject to change without notice. Please allow six to eight weeks for delivery.

Name_____
Address_____
City_____State/Zip_____
Telephone No._____   AB 0596

THE MAGIC CONTINUES...
WITH
LYNNE REID BANKS

THE INDIAN IN THE CUPBOARD
60012-9/$4.50 US/$6.50 Can

THE RETURN OF THE INDIAN   70284-3/$3.99 US

THE SECRET OF THE INDIAN   71040-4/$4.50 US

THE MYSTERY OF THE CUPBOARD
72013-2/$4.50 US/$6.50 Can

I, HOUDINI   70649-0/$4.50 US

THE FAIRY REBEL   70650-4/$4.50 US

THE FARTHEST-AWAY MOUNTAIN
71303-9/$4.50 US

ONE MORE RIVER   71563-5/$3.99 US

THE ADVENTURES OF KING MIDAS
71564-3/$4.50 US

THE MAGIC HARE   71562-7/$5.99 US

Buy these books at your local bookstore or use this coupon for ordering:

Mail to: Avon Books, Dept BP, Box 767, Rte 2, Dresden, TN 38225   E
Please send me the book(s) I have checked above.
❑ My check or money order—no cash or CODs please—for $_____is enclosed (please add $1.50 per order to cover postage and handling—Canadian residents add 7% GST).
❑ Charge my VISA/MC Acct#_____Exp Date_____
Minimum credit card order is two books or $7.50 (please add postage and handling charge of $1.50 per order—Canadian residents add 7% GST). For faster service, call 1-800-762-0779. Residents of Tennessee, please call 1-800-633-1607. Prices and numbers are subject to change without notice. Please allow six to eight weeks for delivery.

Name_____
Address_____
City_____State/Zip_____
Telephone No._____   LRB 0396

Join in the Wild and Crazy Adventures with Some Trouble-Making Plants

by Nancy McArthur

THE PLANT THAT ATE DIRTY SOCKS
75493-2/ $3.99 US/ $5.50 Can

THE RETURN OF THE PLANT THAT ATE DIRTY SOCKS
75873-3/ $3.99 US/ $5.50 Can

THE ESCAPE OF THE PLANT THAT ATE DIRTY SOCKS
76756-2/ $3.50 US/ $4.25 Can

THE SECRET OF THE PLANT THAT ATE DIRTY SOCKS
76757-0/ $3.99 US/ $4.99 Can

MORE ADVENTURES OF THE PLANT THAT ATE DIRTY SOCKS
77663-4/ $3.99 US/ $4.99 Can

THE PLANT THAT ATE DIRTY SOCKS GOES UP IN SPACE
77664-2/ $3.99 US/ $5.50 Can

THE MYSTERY OF THE PLANT THAT ATE DIRTY SOCKS
78318-5/ $3.99 US/ $4.99 Can

Buy these books at your local bookstore or use this coupon for ordering:

Mail to: Avon Books, Dept BP, Box 767, Rte 2, Dresden, TN 38225   E
Please send me the book(s) I have checked above.
❑ My check or money order—no cash or CODs please—for $_____is enclosed (please add $1.50 per order to cover postage and handling—Canadian residents add 7% GST).
❑ Charge my VISA/MC Acct#_____Exp Date_____
Minimum credit card order is two books or $7.50 (please add postage and handling charge of $1.50 per order—Canadian residents add 7% GST). For faster service, call 1-800-762-0779. Residents of Tennessee, please call 1-800-633-1607. Prices and numbers are subject to change without notice. Please allow six to eight weeks for delivery.

Name_____
Address_____
City_____State/Zip_____
Telephone No._____   ESC 0596

JOIN IN THE FUN IN THE WACKY WORLD OF WAYSIDE SCHOOL
by
LOUIS SACHAR

SIDEWAYS STORIES FROM WAYSIDE SCHOOL
69871-4/ $4.50 US/ $5.99 Can

Anything can happen in a school that was all mixed up from the day it was built.

WAYSIDE SCHOOL IS FALLING DOWN
75484-3/ $4.50 US/ $5.99 Can

All the kids in Miss Jewls' class help turn each day into one madcap adventure after another.

WAYSIDE SCHOOL GETS A LITTLE STRANGER
72381-6/ $4.50 US/ $6.50 Can

Also by
Louis Sachar

JOHNNY'S IN THE BASEMENT
83451-0/ $4.50 US/ $6.50 Can

SOMEDAY ANGELINE
83444-8/ $4.50 US/ $6.50 Can

Buy these books at your local bookstore or use this coupon for ordering:
....

Mail to: Avon Books, Dept BP, Box 767, Rte 2, Dresden, TN 38225   E
Please send me the book(s) I have checked above.
❏ My check or money order—no cash or CODs please—for $_____is enclosed (please
add $1.50 per order to cover postage and handling—Canadian residents add 7% GST).
❏ Charge my VISA/MC Acct#_____Exp Date_____
Minimum credit card order is two books or $7.50 (please add postage and handling
charge of $1.50 per order—Canadian residents add 7% GST). For faster service, call
1-800-762-0779. Residents of Tennessee, please call 1-800-633-1607. Prices and numbers are
subject to change without notice. Please allow six to eight weeks for delivery.

Name_____
Address_____
City_____State/Zip_____
Telephone No._____   LS 0596